Gabrielle floated back to Crystals in her
new primrose robe, with her lovely wings
helping her to drift along the corridors. The
moonstones that trimmed her gown seemed to
Gabrielle like the prettiest of raindrops, and
she couldn't stop glancing at them and
touching their smooth surface. With the
wonderful gown and beautiful wings, she
was beginning to feel like a proper angel.

First published in the UK in 2013 by Usborne Publishing Ltd.,
Usborne House, 83-85 Saffron Hill, London EC1N 8RT, England.
www.usborne.com

Illustrations by Antonia Miller.

This is a work of fiction. The characters, incidents, and dialogues are products of
the author's imagination and are not to be construed as real. Any resemblance
to actual events or persons, living or dead, is entirely coincidental.

A CIP catalogue record for this book is available from the British Library.

JF AMJJASOND/13 ISBN 9781409538608 02819/1
Printed in Reading, Berkshire, UK.

ANGEL ACADEMY

Wings and Wishes

Janey Louise Jones

USBORNE

Chapter 1

Gabrielle Divine's heart fluttered with
excitement. At last, the big day had arrived.
She was about to leave her earthly home
and family behind, and start her new life at
a very unusual boarding school far across
the sky, in the world of Cloud Nimbus.
Gabrielle was heading to Angel Academy,
where she would learn how to become a
Guardian Angel.

She didn't know of any other girls lucky enough to be invited to train at Angel Academy. She was nervous about starting her new school without a friend, but even so, she couldn't wait to get there.

Gabrielle took the school's kit list out of the back pocket of her jeans one last time to check again that she'd packed everything:

birth certificate, halo, enrolment papers, rule book, next-of-kin details, washbag, nightwear

"Are you ready, Gabrielle?" called Dad. "It's time to go."

"Just coming, Dad," she replied.

Gabrielle looked at herself in the oval mirror on her white dressing table. Her shoulder-length chestnut brown hair had just been trimmed at the India Rose salon on the High Street. Her heart-shaped face had the faintest hint of pink flush in the cheeks and her blue-green eyes were sparkling.

Gabrielle had finally decided to wear her favourite jeans and her pink baseball boots for the journey to Cloud Nimbus. And she'd put on the new jacket Mum had made her, which she adored. It was cherry-pink velvet, cropped short at the waist, and decorated with turquoise patchwork flowers.

It said in the school rule book that "angelic gowns" would be given to all new students on arrival at Angel Academy and Gabrielle couldn't wait to see them. She wondered if they'd be made from soft white silk with gold edging, like the one worn by the very first angel who had visited her.

Although that had been a long time ago, it was still perfectly clear in Gabrielle's mind.

It had all begun on Christmas Eve, four years earlier – a cold, crisp winter's evening, when frosty sparkles lay across the grass in the Divines' moonlit garden.

Gabrielle had been seven years old at the time. She was a small girl, with plump cheeks and a high ponytail, and she wore an emerald green woollen coat and purple tights. As she ran up to the top of the garden in her short pink wellies, looking for Father Christmas and his reindeer in the sky, she'd felt as if there was pure magic in the freezing air. Suddenly, out of nowhere, a delicate angel had appeared, standing on the naked branch of a bony tree.

The angel had beautiful feathery wings, and a gleaming golden halo shone above her head. Her kind eyes were like  rich pools of liquid chocolate. She bore a gift. It was hidden inside a glittering golden box, tied with ribbons of ivory satin.

"Hello, Gabrielle Divine," the angel said. "I'm Angel Fleur. Don't be afraid. I have come to tell you about your future. You've been chosen by the great Madame Seraph to train as a Guardian Angel."

Angel Fleur had fluttered down to where Gabrielle stood and handed her the golden box.

"Treasure the gift inside this box," the angel said. "When you're eleven, we hope you will join us at Angel Academy where your training will begin. Only your mother and father can know of this. In the meantime, spread your peaceful angel spirit wherever you go. Merry Christmas, dear Gabrielle."

With that, Angel Fleur had disappeared into the night sky.

Gabrielle remembered wondering whether she had imagined it all – and yet the box in her hands had been real.

Her mother had been standing in the

doorway, smiling at what she had seen. "When you were born, an angel appeared and told me this would happen," she said softly. "But I didn't believe the day would come so soon."

 Gabrielle had undone the ribbons around the box and lifted the lid, her eyes growing wide with astonishment. Inside had been a beautiful halo, made from purest gold and set with smooth, milky moonstones. It hadn't glowed at first, but when she tried it on, it seemed to gain energy and a bright light shone from it. She knew then that she hadn't imagined the angel's visit.

"You look beautiful. I'm so proud of you," Mum had said, with glistening eyes.

* * *

Over the next few years, occasional messages were sent to the Divines from Angel Academy, but Gabrielle hadn't given a great deal of thought to Angel Fleur's words. Her childhood had been a normal, earthly one.

Gabrielle had not even discussed Angel Academy much with her parents until her eleventh birthday approached. Then they talked it through often and it was especially hard for Dad to understand. He had always known that his wife's mother was an angel, but he hadn't imagined that one day their child would become an angel too and be invited to live far away in the clouds.

At her eleventh birthday party sleepover, some of Gabrielle's friends had spotted the golden box at the back of a cupboard in her room and before she could do anything about it, they'd found the halo inside.

"Wow! Look at this!" Georgie said, lifting it from its box.

"Hey, Gabrielle. I never knew you had one of these," Evie cooed.

"It's gorgeous," Freya added. "Let me try it on! Please."

Oh, please don't let them find out it's a real angel's halo. I'll never be able to explain, Gabrielle had thought nervously. She remembered biting her lip as they'd played around with it. But it hadn't risen up and started glowing when her friends tried it on. Instead it sat flat on their heads, like a halo from a fancy-dress shop.

Gabrielle could remember the moment

quite clearly. That experience had taught her that she was different – and that she'd always have to keep secrets from her earthly friends.

Since her birthday, the visits from the angels had increased. And finally, one spring evening, Angel Academy's Head Angel, Madame Seraph herself, had arrived at the Divines' house. She had floated gracefully into their back garden, as they sat out in the early spring sunshine. Landing gently on the lawn, Madame Seraph had explained that she hoped Gabrielle would come to Angel Academy at the start of the new school year.

Gabrielle had thought the angel was amazing; wise and beautiful and, most of all, kind.

"What is it about Gabrielle that makes you want to train her?" Mum asked.

"She is very special," Madame Seraph had replied, "as she has incredibly strong human qualities, combined with your mother's excellent angel characteristics. Your mother was a very fine Guardian Angel."

"Was?" said Mum.

"Yes. I'm so sorry, my dear." Madame Seraph paused. "I'm afraid she died of a broken heart because she couldn't be with you," she said softly.

"Oh no!" Mum sobbed. Dad had placed his arm around her protectively and Gabrielle had run to her side.

"You know your mother would have

been in touch if she'd been alive, don't you?" Dad said gently.

Mum nodded.

Madame Seraph explained what had happened. "Angels cannot live on Earth for ever. That's why she had to return to her angel home, leaving you to be raised by your father. But she missed you so much."

"Dad misses her to this day," Mum said. "He talked about her all the time when I was growing up."

"She was one of the best Guardian Angels we've ever had. But all of your mother's talents can be well used through Gabrielle," Madame Seraph said. "Both you and Gabrielle can live in either world, as part-angels. If Gabrielle comes to Angel Academy, she will be cherished and you can trust me to protect her. She will have such an exciting future. Angel Academy is a school full of love and kindness."

After Madame Seraph had left, the Divines sat in stunned silence. But Gabrielle had already made up her mind that she wanted to go to Angel Academy. She wanted to feel close to her grandmother and she knew she would be safe with Madame Seraph.

"Please let me go to Angel Academy," she'd pleaded with her mum and dad. "I want to follow in Granny's footsteps and become a Guardian Angel like she was."

And although Gabrielle's parents had worried that she would find the new school strange, they didn't try to stop her because they saw that she wanted to go to Angel Academy more than anything else in the world.

Chapter 2

"Gabrielle Divine! I'll not tell you again," called Dad, from downstairs. "We're definitely going to be late."

"Sorry! Just coming now," Gabrielle replied, fastening a bead bracelet round her wrist.

The Angel Academy rule book mentioned that she would be given a Guardian Angel charm bracelet, and she'd

have to earn the charms for it by learning
the special skills she needed to become a
Guardian Angel. Would the charms be
gold, or silver…made from moonstones, or
delicate crystals? They sparkled and spun
in her mind's eye, like exquisite fragments
of purest starlight.

It was exciting thoughts like these which
helped her to leave her safe and pretty little
attic bedroom, knowing she would not be
back until Christmas. *I'm going to miss this
place so much*, she thought, closing the door
behind her.

Dad put Gabrielle's bag in the boot of
the car, then the Divine family jumped in,
and set off for Gabrielle's departure point
in Featherwing Woods.

"D'you think I'll ever learn how to be a

Guardian Angel?" she asked, suddenly
unsure of what awaited her on Cloud
Nimbus. "I'll have to pass loads of tests
to earn the charms for my bracelet."

"You'll get them all," said Mum. "I'm
sure Madame Seraph will teach you well.
You're going to be brilliant… Do it for me."

Gabrielle was thoughtful for a moment.
Then she took a deep breath and asked the
question she had never liked to ask before:
"Why did you never go to Angel Academy,
Mum?"

Clara Divine smiled and her eyes grew
misty for a moment. "Oh, it was my dearest
wish when I was your age," she said. "But
for me it just wasn't possible."

"Why not?" Gabrielle asked.

"Grandpa was so sad after Granny had

to leave," said Mum. "I know he would have let me go, but it would have broken his heart for a second time, and I couldn't let that happen."

Gabrielle took hold of her mum's hand and squeezed it gently. "Then I'll do it for both of us," she said. "I'll make you so proud."

"We're here," said Dad, interrupting their conversation. He pulled the car over onto a grass verge and they all got out.

"What do I do now?" asked Gabrielle.

"It says in this letter that we should take you to the middle of Featherwing Woods, and you will be transported to the world of Cloud Nimbus from there," said Dad.

"I'm scared," said Gabrielle, grabbing her mother's hand. It was too awful to think about saying goodbye to both her parents, but Gabrielle and her mum were especially close. Lovely, kind, gentle Clara Divine was the best mother in the world.

"You don't have to do this…" said Dad, with a note of hope in his voice.

But since Madame Seraph's visit, Gabrielle had dreamed many times of having wings and flying across the sky, of wearing an angelic gown and making friends with other angels – and of completing her charm bracelet. Now that the magical moment had arrived, she couldn't let it go.

"I want to do it," she said, sounding more confident than she felt.

As they stepped through the woods, the trees seemed to take on a bright quality, as though bathed in golden light. The Divines didn't need the directions attached to the letter; they simply followed the trail of angel feathers that fluttered in front of them, floating just above the ground.

There were sounds that led them on too; somewhere in the distance magical harp strings plucked a gentle tune.

As the music grew louder, the light became brighter. Dad gave Gabrielle her bag and stood back, realizing that this was the moment he had to let go, but Mum remained protectively by Gabrielle's side.

Gabrielle looked at her mother's familiar face; all warm, smiley and freckly. Her wavy

brown hair was held back in a ponytail
and her slim frame was enveloped in a floral
wrap-around dress.

As they embraced, Gabrielle breathed
in her mum's perfume – vanilla and roses –
a scent that felt so comforting. Tears
streamed down both their faces.

"I'll miss you, darling," said Mum.

"I'll miss you too. You'll definitely come
to Parents' Day though, won't you?"
sobbed Gabrielle.

"Of course I will. Try keeping me away.
I can't wait to see you at Angel Academy,"
said Mum.

"I'll write with all my news," said Gabrielle.

Mum nodded through her tears, and
stroked her daughter's soft chestnut hair.
Suddenly, a flash of golden light dazzled

them. They each raised a hand to shield their eyes, and as they grew accustomed to the brilliant light, they saw an incredible vision standing before them. It was a magnificent, winged angel horse, with a halo glowing above his noble head. He looked at Gabrielle with such kind brown eyes that she couldn't be afraid of him.

"Gabrielle Divine, I am Domino, your chevalange. I will take you safely to Cloud Nimbus," he said, in a rich, velvety voice, which echoed majestically through the trees.

"Erm, th-thank you," she stammered.

The angel horse turned to Mum. "Do not fear, Mrs. Divine. Everyone at the Academy has a chevalange as a partner. I am Gabrielle's. She will be safe with me.

And I will return to collect you and Mr.
Divine for Parents' Day in a few weeks."

"Thank you," said Mum.

"Now, Gabrielle, say goodbye to your
parents and climb up on my back," Domino
said. Gabrielle turned towards Mum and
Dad for the last time. Dad moved forward,
holding Mum close to him.

"Bye," she cried, running to embrace
them both. "I'll miss you."

"And we'll miss you, little angel," said
Dad in a sad, broken voice.

Mum couldn't speak through her tears,
but she kissed Gabrielle one last time.

Before she could change her mind,
Gabrielle put her bag on her back, climbed
onto Domino and took hold of the reins.

"Hold on tightly," the chevalange said.

"There will be time for proper riding lessons at Angel Academy." He flapped his vast wings and they quickly became airborne, climbing with great speed above the trees of Featherwing Woods, towards the angel world.

Part of her wanted to ask Domino to turn back, but Gabrielle knew she had to fulfil her angel dreams. She waved to her parents and blinked away the tears. After that, she didn't look back – the separation was too painful. But she felt safe and Domino reassured her with soft whinnies. She looked ahead and wondered what the world of Cloud Nimbus would hold for her.

Chapter 3

As they rose higher and higher, Gabrielle's hair blew in the gentle breeze, and she could sense that the air was changing around her, becoming purer and clearer.

She loved the feeling of riding and flying at the same time and didn't want the magical journey to end, but before long, Domino turned his head towards her. "Nearly there!" he said.

Nothing could have prepared Gabrielle for their arrival in Cloud Nimbus. From a distance, it looked like no more than a fluffy, white cotton-wool cloud. But as they entered it, passing through many layers of sparkling crystal drops, a whole world opened up, enveloped by soft hills.

"Would you like to see more of Cloud Nimbus before we land?" asked Domino.

"Oh, I would love that, thank you," said Gabrielle.

They swooped off to the west, and Domino talked her through all that was beneath them. As they came to the heart of Cloud Nimbus, Gabrielle saw a beautiful city unfolding below them and wondered about the grandmother she had never met, who had lived here for most of her life.

"This is the main town, which we call Bliss," he explained. "There are traders' stalls within it, selling fruits, herbs, jewels, minerals and perfumes. Oh, and the chocolate shop is a must. And see, before the river, there are wondrous homes where angel families live."

Gabrielle gasped. The angels' mansions below looked like intricately iced wedding cakes.

Next, it was time to view the school, located in the centre of the town.

"Here it is – the famous Angel Academy," said Domino proudly.

It was breathtaking – a white, turreted, fairy-tale castle. There were archways leading into a central courtyard, with

towers at each corner. A large white and
gold flag fluttered from one of the towers,
and a vast lake shimmered in the beautiful
grounds.

Domino flew across the lake and
prepared to land. Gabrielle looked down
and saw many angels in the grounds,
linking arms and chatting happily. Some
flew about, while others hovered just above
the ground. They wore
wonderful angelic gowns,
with fragile wings fluttering
behind them, and golden
halos glowing on their heads.

"They are all in their angelic gowns
already," observed Gabrielle.

"Don't worry. Soon, you will look just
the same," said Domino.

"Great!" said Gabrielle, longing to be just like the others. "But I don't have any wings."

"Madame Seraph will see to everything," he said.

Gabrielle couldn't wait to see Madame Seraph again. "She was so kind when she came to visit," said Gabrielle. "Is she always like that?"

"Yes, she's eternally kind," said Domino. He landed gently on the lawn in front of the school and Gabrielle jumped down.

Domino looked as if he was going to take off again, and Gabrielle panicked. So far, he was her only link with the new world.

"Where are you going?" she asked.

"Back to the paddock, for a rest," he smiled. "Go up to the main door ahead and you will be met by one of the teachers."

"When will I see you again?" asked Gabrielle.

"Whenever you like. We are bonded now. I will be your partner for the whole time you're at the Academy. You can visit me at any time for advice or just to chat. One day, we will go to Earth together on Guardian Angel missions," he said. "But that's a long way off. You'll have several years of training first."

"Thank you for everything, Domino. Bye for now," she said.

Domino rose up into the air and Gabrielle felt a comforting cool breeze around her as he flapped his wings.

She waved him off and made her way nervously up to the main entrance. Sure enough, there was an angel waiting for her, at a huge doorway which was set into a softly curving, chalky white archway.

The angel's face was familiar, and so warm and welcoming that Gabrielle felt instantly at ease. It was Angel Fleur – the angel who'd given Gabrielle her halo in the golden box on Christmas Eve four years earlier.

"Welcome to Angel Academy, Gabrielle," the angel smiled kindly. "I'm Fleur, and I teach here. We've met once before of course – in your garden, if you remember. How was your journey?"

"It was brilliant, thanks," said Gabrielle, excitedly. "And of course I remember you." She looked at Fleur's stunning silken robe and its intriguing embroidered symbols with awe. She knew she was going to love every detail of the angel world.

"Leave your bag here and it will be taken to your room. Come this way," said Fleur. "Madame Seraph awaits us in the gardens."

Gabrielle felt she would burst with pride. The great Madame Seraph was waiting for her?

Gabrielle's throat was dry with nerves as she followed Fleur down a wide corridor. The walls were a warm amber colour and the windows were open, letting in light and cool, fresh air.

Fleur led her through open French doors into a lovely cobbled courtyard, filled with tubs of sweet-smelling herbs and white, lacy flowers. They walked

through a gate into scented gardens.

"This is where you will learn the art of Potion-making," said Fleur. "We need secret potions to help soothe humans in distress. Come this way."

Gabrielle thought that making potions sounded wonderful.

"Ah! Angel Gabrielle," said a voice from above. "How delightful to see you again!"

Gabrielle looked up and saw the impressive Madame Seraph flying gracefully overhead.

She landed softly right beside them, and Gabrielle admired her dewy skin and her bright sky-blue eyes. Madame Seraph's Guardian Angel bracelet was also glorious. Twelve enchanting charms dangled from it, glittering and sparkling in the sunlight.

"Welcome, Gabrielle. We're delighted to have you here," said Madame Seraph, "and we have high hopes for you. Fleur will give you a tour of the rest of the school, and then you will be fitted for your gowns. I will wish your wings upon you, and then you will take the Angel Oath with the other new trainee Guardian Angels. We call you all Cherubics. How does that sound?"

For a moment, Gabrielle was unable to speak – she felt a little overwhelmed in Madame Seraph's presence.

"Erm, lovely," she managed at last.

"We've waited many years for you to come here, Gabrielle. We believe you are totally exceptional," said the Head Angel.

"I am?" She wondered what Madame Seraph meant. She felt confused, yet elated and proud, all at once. But her thoughts were interrupted as the Head Angel spoke again.

"I have other matters to attend to now, but I'll see you again very soon."

After saying goodbye to Madame Seraph, Gabrielle walked and Fleur floated quietly back to the main school building.

"What do you think so far?" asked Fleur.

"Amazing," said Gabrielle, still wondering about Madame Seraph's words. Plucking up the courage, she said, "Excuse me for asking, but why did Madame say I was 'totally exceptional'?"

"Because she sees the most wonderful angel and human qualities in you," said Angel Fleur. "Madame will tell you more about it later. Let's see some of the departments of Angel Charms now," smiled Fleur.

They swept along many corridors, and it seemed to Gabrielle that each new department they visited was more interesting than the last. She saw that she would learn Angelfly Dancing, and the Art of Vanishing, plus Potion-making, Messenger Skills and Angel Wishing.

Such care was taken with every little detail at Angel Academy. Gabrielle gazed at glass cabinets filled with jars of sparkling crystals. She noticed shiny trumpets, wonderful lutes and delicate harps, and elsewhere there were rows of dainty satin shoes for Angelfly Dancing.

"Everything's so beautiful," said Gabrielle.

"We need all these lovely things," said Fleur, "to teach you the Angel Charms."

"They're perfect," said Gabrielle.

"Ah, I'm afraid things aren't always perfect here," said Fleur. "After all, we're training you to be Guardian Angels – and it takes time to master perfection! Come on, I'll show you to your room; it's called Crystals. And I'll introduce you to the other new Cherubics who will live with you. There's Ruth Bell, and the twins, Charity and Hope Honeychurch."

Gabrielle couldn't wait to meet some other angels of her own age for the first time. And yet she couldn't help but worry. *Will they be very different from my friends at home?* she asked herself.

Chapter 4

When Gabrielle walked through the door
of Crystals, a girl wearing an elegant pale-
blue gown came rushing towards her. Wild
red curls bounced on her head. She had a
kind and open face, and dancing dark eyes;
she seemed a very warm-hearted angel.

"Hi, I'm Ruth Bell," said the girl.

"Hello, I'm Gabrielle Divine."

"Nice clothes. I like your hair. Are you

looking forward to this term? I'm not.
I arrived earlier today and it's been rubbish
so far," said Ruth, without stopping for
breath. "And if you're wondering where our
room-mates are, they're at a gown-fitting
with Angel Willow. Bo-ring!"

Gabrielle stopped in her tracks,
delighted to meet her bubbly room-mate,
but surprised that she seemed far from
enchanted by her new surroundings.

"Oh, Ruth!" said Fleur, with a smile.
"You'll both love it here! But I'm afraid
I've got to go and get ready for the
ceremony now."

"Thanks for showing me round," said
Gabrielle.

"It's been a pleasure. Ruth, remember
you are going to help collect flowers from

the garden to decorate the main hall for
the Oath-taking Ceremony, when the sun
is directly over Bliss. And Gabrielle, here's
a copy of your timetable. You have some
important appointments later on this
afternoon: a fitting for gowns, wing-
wishing, and the Oath-taking Ceremony,
of course. Don't be late!"

The new room-mates said goodbye to
Fleur, and Gabrielle began to unpack her
bag which had been left on her bed for her.
She noticed beautiful silver stands on the
bedside tables, which she guessed were for
their halos. Everyone she'd seen so far
wore a halo, so she took her own from its
box in her bag and placed it on her head.

"Do we need to wear our halos all the
time?" she asked.

"We take them off at night, but we wouldn't have some of our angel powers without them," said Ruth, looking puzzled. "You know, just like at home."

"I see," said Gabrielle, grateful that she had a halo already, but aware that Ruth clearly thought she should know more about them.

She looked at her room-mate's simple, pale-blue tunic-gown, trimmed with tiny feathers and ivory seed pearls, and suddenly her clothes felt all wrong.

"I love your gown," said Gabrielle.

"I prefer your clothes. Where did you get them?" asked Ruth.

"Um, well, Mum made the jacket for me and the jeans are from a shop at home," said Gabrielle.

"And where's that?" asked Ruth.

"Oxford."

"You mean on Earth?" said Ruth, wide-eyed.

"Erm…" said Gabrielle.

"No way!" cried Ruth, dancing up and down excitedly. "I wondered why you didn't have wings and asked about halos. Wow! You're an Earth Angel! That's incredible!"

"Oh, is it?" said Gabrielle, confused by Ruth's reaction.

"Yes, it's amazing. I thought Earth Angels were a myth," said Ruth. "Oooh, I'm longing to go to Earth. It sounds brilliant! Why would you want to come here when you live on Earth?"

Gabrielle was taken aback by Ruth's

question. "But I think Angel Academy is wonderful," she said. "I want to learn to be a Guardian Angel."

"I can't believe this," Ruth carried on. "D'you have any angel skills? Does it feel weird, being a bit of both – angel and human?"

"Erm, I don't know any different," admitted Gabrielle, who was starting to feel a little freaky.

"Don't worry. It's a great thing that you're unusual," said Ruth. "My grandmother told me about Earth Angels. It means you have earthly and angelic talents. Where does your angel blood come from?" asked Ruth.

"From my mother," said Gabrielle. "She's half-angel. She stayed on Earth as a child and didn't come to Angel Academy. But my granny was a full-angel and had to come back to Cloud Nimbus, even though she married Grandpa, who is human."

"Where's your granny now?" asked Ruth.

"Madame Seraph told us that she died," Gabrielle explained.

"Oh, that's sad, I'm sorry," said Ruth.

"It's okay," said Gabrielle. "It's sad for my mum."

"Yes, it must be hard for her to be part-angel, yet never do any angel stuff," said Ruth.

"I don't think she knows how to do any angel stuff," said Gabrielle.

"Ooh," said Ruth suddenly. "Look at the sun – I need to help collect the flowers now. Why don't you settle in? I'll try to be as quick as I can."

The room was quiet without Ruth, and Gabrielle had a lot to think about. She sat on her bed in a daze as she took on board the astonishing fact that she was different from all the other trainee Guardian Angels. Now she knew why Madame Seraph had called her "totally exceptional" – it was because she was an Earth Angel – though she still didn't really understand exactly what that meant.

Gabrielle had butterflies in her tummy. *I guess there's no one on Earth like me, and no one on Cloud Nimbus like me either,* she thought. *So much for wanting to be just like all the other angels!*

The sound of sweet birdsong at the

window made Gabrielle look around. A pretty white dove with silver and pink markings was peeping in at her.

"Hello," said the bird. "I don't mean to interrupt your thoughts. I'm Sylvie. I'm the messenger dove for you and your room-mates in Crystals."

Gabrielle had never met a talking bird before. She was stunned for a moment,  but the little bird was so adorable and she didn't want to be rude. "Oh, hello, Sylvie," she said. "Come in."

The beautiful bird flew over to Gabrielle and landed on her outstretched hand. "Nice to meet you, Gabrielle," she said. "I'll always be on your windowsill, unless I'm away on an errand for someone."

"Oh, that's amazing!" Gabrielle smiled. Their own messenger dove! Angel Academy was certainly full of surprises.

"Am I imagining it, or did I hear that you're an Earth Angel?" said Sylvie.

"Apparently I am," said Gabrielle.

"It's an honour to meet you," said Sylvie. "I never thought I'd see the day!"

"Wow! An honour to meet me?" said Gabrielle. "I feel the same way about you."

Sylvie chirped and flew back to the windowsill.

Ruth burst back into the room, carrying a posy of perfumed white roses. "We picked too many flowers for the hall, so I thought I'd bring these back for us," she said, putting them in a vase.

"Mmm. Don't they smell lovely?" said

Gabrielle, having to fight back
the tears that threatened
to fall. "They remind
me of my mum."

"Oh," said Ruth. "Why is that?"

Gabrielle paused. Ruth would think it
silly. But she decided to tell the truth.
"Mum's favourite perfume smells of vanilla
and roses," she said, pulling a scarf from her
bag. "This is Mum's. It's sprayed with her
perfume. I brought it with me to remind me
of home."

"Oh, please don't cry," said Ruth,
looking anxious. "I'm still feeling cross with
my mum. I didn't want to come here. But
she said I had to. It's a family tradition. My
Granny Bell is one of the Governors here.
Lah-di-dah. Who cares about all that?"

Gabrielle thought that Ruth's family must be very important at Angel Academy. To Gabrielle, this whole new world was endlessly intriguing, but Ruth seemed to take it for granted, because she'd grown up knowing all about it. Not sure quite what to say next, Gabrielle changed the subject.

"What are our two room-mates like?" she asked.

"They seem okay. One's dreamy and one's sensible, so they make a pretty good team," said Ruth. "But don't ask me which is which."

"They sound nice," said Gabrielle. Then she caught sight of herself in the mirror.

She longed to be dressed like Ruth, and she looked at the appointment card Fleur had given her. "Gown-fitting at Sun Dip?"

she mumbled, nonplussed. "What does that mean?"

"Most times of the day are described by the position of the sun or moon on Cloud Nimbus," explained Ruth. "Sun Dip means when the sun disappears over the hill behind Bliss."

"Oh. Okay, thanks," said Gabrielle.

"Don't worry, I'll tell you when to go," said Ruth. "And we can go to the Oath-taking Ceremony together and then down to tea, if you like? I sat all alone at lunch and it was miserable."

"Great, I'd like that. Is the food good?" asked Gabrielle.

"Yes, it's pretty nice, actually. We had a great pudding," said Ruth, suddenly sounding really enthusiastic. "It was called

Angel's Fool, and it had sweet berries, ice cream and meringue, with this chewy toffee glaze over the top. Scrummy!"

"Yum," said Gabrielle. She and Ruth were very different, but Gabrielle couldn't help liking her new room-mate. And she had the feeling that they would become the best of friends.

Chapter 5

"It's time for you to go to the gown department!" said Ruth, interrupting Gabrielle's thoughts some time later. "I'll take you if you like!"

"Oh yes, please," said Gabrielle. "I've no idea where I'm supposed to go."

"Come on then," she said, bounding out of the door. "I'm so glad that you're in my room," she continued as she floated along the corridor beside Gabrielle.

"Me too," said Gabrielle, watching Ruth as she moved. "You're floating, but I'm walking," she commented.

"I expect you'll learn to float and fly soon enough!" said Ruth. "Once you have your wings."

The gown department was bustling with activity. There were six private fitting rooms, with plum-coloured velvet curtains. An angel dashed about with a measuring tape around her neck and a pincushion in one hand, as new trainee Guardian Angels admired their reflections in long mirrors edged with ornate gold frames.

"I've already been through all this, so I'd better keep out of Angel Willow's way," said Ruth.

"Thanks, Ruth. I'll see you later," said Gabrielle. As she walked further into the room she gasped at the sight of row upon row of delicate-coloured gowns hanging in the open wardrobes. The trimmings and accessories were eye-catching too: shelves full of braiding, feathers, moonstones, gems, sequins, beads, pearls and lace.

As Gabrielle took in the scene, she noticed that Madame Seraph had come in and was hovering by the wardrobes.

"Gabrielle, let's sit for a moment and chat," said Madame.

Gabrielle did as she was told.

"Gabrielle," said the Head Angel, "as I mentioned earlier, you are exceptional; an angel quite different from the rest of us.

Don't be alarmed by this. As an Earth Angel you have human and angel blood combined, so do not fear your differences. You are very special."

"But I don't have any wings yet. You said something about wishing them on me but I don't really understand…" said Gabrielle.

"That is something I am going to attend to as soon as you have been fitted for gowns. Please don't worry, it's quite simple and it will cause no discomfort whatsoever," Madame Seraph explained.

"Oh, thank you," gasped Gabrielle. "I can't wait!"

"Madame," called Angel Willow. "May I get on with measuring Gabrielle now?"

"Of course. I will wait here until you have finished with her," said Madame.

The tall, glamorous Angel Willow, was running her fingers through Gabrielle's hair. "You're the last of the day," she said kindly. "We don't have long before Oath-taking, so let's get started."

Once her hair was styled around her halo, Gabrielle stood completely still as Willow measured her, and held different swatches of fabric against her face. "I think I know just what to pick," she said.

Gabrielle was delighted when Angel Willow gave her three stylishly trimmed dresses to wear: one primrose yellow, soft to the touch and decorated with moonstones, another pale turquoise and a third blush-pink. Gabrielle chose to wear the primrose-coloured one, and carried the other two over her arm. Next Willow

draped a white velvet cloak over Gabrielle's
shoulders and slipped a gorgeous pair of
satin ballet-style pumps on her feet. She
also gave her a pair of the softest leather
boots in a silken bag. Gabrielle looked
almost the same as the others now – except
for the wings.

Madame gazed proudly at Gabrielle in
her angel clothes. "Step forward, Angel
Gabrielle," she said.

As Gabrielle moved forward, a
marvellous light glowed around Madame
Seraph and a whoosh of energy came from
her, towards Gabrielle.

As the Head Angel
spread her own wings
out fully and hovered
above her, Gabrielle's

feet lifted and she began to spin around. She felt a warm, tingling sensation between her shoulders. When she turned her head, she saw a beautiful pair of feathery white wings were emerging from her shoulder blades.

Madame Seraph continued to circle above her as the new wings fluttered gently and grew to their full size.

Finally, Madame came back to ground level and took Gabrielle's hands as she floated with her new wings flapping softly behind her.

"How do they feel?" asked Madame.

"Lovely!" said Gabrielle, as Madame Seraph let go of her and she floated around the room. "This is fun!"

"Now, do remember that it will be a while before you can fly outdoors with the others," said Madame. "So, please be very careful."

"I will," said Gabrielle. "Can I go and show Ruth?"

"Of course. And I will see you soon, at the Oath-taking Ceremony!"

Gabrielle floated back to Crystals in her new primrose robe, with her lovely wings helping her to drift along the corridors. The moonstones that trimmed her gown seemed to Gabrielle like the prettiest of raindrops, and she couldn't stop glancing at them and touching their smooth surface. With the wonderful gown and beautiful wings, she was beginning to feel like a proper angel.

When she arrived back at Crystals, Hope and Charity were there.

"Hi, Gabrielle!" they called brightly, in unison. They both had light-brown hair, but one wore pigtails, while the other wore her hair loosely brushed over her shoulders.

"Hello. Ooh, you have lovely gowns too," said Gabrielle.

"Yes, we asked if we could each have slightly different colours and designs, otherwise it's hard to tell us apart," said one of the twins, showing off her sleeves, which were scalloped while her sister's were plain. "But really, we're very different. I'm Hope and I've got green eyes."

"And I'm Charity and mine are dark brown," said her sister.

Gabrielle went closer to look. "I see what you mean," she smiled. "I'll try not to mix you up."

"Ruth told us you're an Earth Angel," said Hope. "That's exciting!"

"I didn't know until today," said Gabrielle.

"She's got great Earth clothes," said Ruth.

"I love this gown, actually," Gabrielle said, looking down at her new dress. "What did you all wear before you came to Angel Academy?"

"Girl angels on Cloud Nimbus wear gowns, but they're not as fancy as these, and boys wear tunics," explained Charity.

"I love hearing about life here," said Gabrielle. "It's all new to me."

"It must be so strange for you," said Hope. "Are you looking forward to the Oath-taking Ceremony?"

"Yes, but I don't really know what it involves," she admitted.

"Me neither," said Hope. "But I'm sure Madame Seraph will make it all seem easy."

"Oh, I hope so," said Gabrielle, feeling a little scared and excited all at the same time.

Chapter 6

A trumpet sounded a short while after the girls finished their unpacking.

"What does that mean?" asked Gabrielle.

"It means it's time for the Oath-taking Ceremony. Hurry up!" chirped Sylvie from the windowsill.

Hope brushed her hair dreamily, staring into space.

"Hope!" said Charity. "Focus!"

The four girls tidied their hair, checked how they looked in their mirrors, and said goodbye to Sylvie. They made their way to the main hall together.

At the front of the hall was a raised platform, adorned with vast vases of white roses. There was a throne-style chair in the centre of the platform and several chairs to either side of it. The new Cherubics were ushered to seats just in front of this platform.

"Great, we'll get a good view of Madame Seraph when she arrives," Gabrielle whispered to Ruth.

"Who cares?" said Ruth, but she looked around the hall curiously, and Gabrielle had the feeling that her new friend was secretly just as excited as she was.

They sat down next to each other on purple velvet chairs, with the twins on the next two seats, and breathed in a heavenly floral perfume as they awaited the arrival of Madame Seraph and the rest of the angel teachers.

Ruth said hello to a couple of girls who walked past. "They were at my prep school in Bliss," she explained. "That's Merry Harper and Fey Lee, they're good fun."

They smiled over at Gabrielle. She was starting to relax; everyone at Angel Academy seemed so nice and friendly.

Three more girls came towards them, and the tall, pretty girl in the middle stopped to chat. "Hi, I'm Lula Spendlove," she said.

Gabrielle stared at the beautiful angel.

She seemed a little older, and already had a few charms on her bracelet to prove it.

Lula had bouncy, long, chocolate-brown hair, and a perfect kitten face, with wide green eyes, long lashes and a button nose.

"Hello," said the four room-mates in unison.

"Good luck, Cherubics! See you around," said Lula. She and her friends turned and hovered back to their seats.

Gabrielle stared after them. She thought Lula was the coolest angel imaginable – and it was so nice of her to wish them luck.

After that, everyone suddenly stood up and fell silent as Madame Seraph floated on to the platform, accompanied by a team of angelic teachers.

Madame's gown for the Oath-taking

Ceremony was completely perfect, made from shimmering white silk.

"Everyone, please be seated," she said. "Welcome one and all to Angel Academy. And a special welcome to our new trainees; our 'Cherubics'. It is our job to teach you to become Guardian Angels to help humans in need. We hope you will connect with your inner angel and excel during your time here with us."

Gabrielle hung on her every word, and she noticed that the twins and even Ruth did the same.

"Your time at Angel Academy is a gift to you," continued Madame Seraph. "Remember that what we want to discover within you is pure love. I want this Academy and its pupils to sing out with

love and understanding for those in need.
This year, we have twenty new
Cherubics, who are each of equal value
to us. However, I want to mention one
in particular, a Cherubic with exceptional
promise, who is especially far from
home. A girl who has travelled all the
way from Earth…"

There was a gasp of surprise in the hall.

Madame Seraph continued. "We are
honoured and delighted to have our very
first Earth Angel with us. An angel who has
unique potential as she already understands
human ways and will come to understand
angel ways equally well. Please stand up,
Angel Gabrielle!"

Gabrielle blushed and got to her feet
awkwardly as Madame continued.

"I want you all to welcome Cherubic Gabrielle Divine most warmly, and help her find her way around. She is very special to us," said the Head Angel.

There was a lot of clapping and cheering and Gabrielle could feel everyone staring at her, which made her blush even more. She was extremely relieved when Madame told her to sit down and announced that it was time for all the new Cherubics to take their oaths.

"Those of you who are new please come to the platform to take your oath, then you'll be given your Angel Charm bracelet," said Madame Seraph.

Gabrielle forgot her embarrassment as she followed the other newcomers to the platform, where each one was given a sheet

of paper with the Angel Oath written on it.
Then they stood together facing Madame
Seraph and said solemnly and in unison, "I
pledge my life to the art of Angel
Guardianship. I will use my gifts wisely and
well for the sake of humans in need."

Next it was time for the bracelets.
Gabrielle was halfway down the line of
trainee angels and she strained to see what
was happening at the front of the queue. It
seemed as though every bracelet was unique.
It was too intriguing! *Oh! What will mine be
like? Please hurry up!* thought Gabrielle.

When it was her turn, Gabrielle took
a deep breath as Madame Seraph opened
a long, rectangular box, covered in velvet of
the deepest lavender. From it, she took the
most exquisite piece of jewellery Gabrielle

had ever seen. It was a bracelet of silver circle links, joined together with tiny moonstones.

Madame Seraph placed the bracelet on Gabrielle's wrist. It felt smooth and cool against her skin. It was secured by a silver bar which was fed through two of the circles. One day each circle would hold a dainty charm.

"Gabrielle, we welcome you to Angel Academy and look forward to the words of your oath being fulfilled," said Madame Seraph, as she handed over the velvet box.

"Thank you," Gabrielle replied. It was her proudest moment and she wished that her parents had been there to share it.

Feeling happy and sad all at the same time, Gabrielle went to sit down again with her new bracelet on her wrist. She touched it again and again, checking that it was real, and her heartbeat quickened as she realized that this was it. Her life as a trainee Guardian Angel had just begun.

Back in Crystals, the Cherubics excitedly showed their new bracelets to Sylvie.

"I love them all!" she declared. "Take good care of them. But now you should go and wash your hands as it's nearly teatime."

"Oh yay, food!" said Gabrielle, suddenly realizing that in all the excitement, she hadn't eaten since this morning. "I'd forgotten about that!"

"Come on, everyone," said Charity as a trumpet sounded, "let's all go to tea together!"

"The Ambroserie refectory is pretty cool," said Ruth, as they floated along many corridors, following the delicious smell of freshly-baked bread.

"I can't wait!" said Gabrielle. "I'm starving."

They turned a corner and there was the Ambroserie. Gabrielle stopped in her tracks for a moment to take in the magnificent scene. The vast dining room was filled with light that streamed in through an enormous domed window in the ceiling. There were large circular tables spaced evenly about the room and the four girls sat down at one. It was abundant with food: warm bread and creamy butter, golden pies, colourful salads, dishes of pasta, delicate cupcakes and perfectly ripe fresh fruits.

To Gabrielle's surprise, Lula and her friends joined the same table.

"Hi again," said Lula, looking at the four friends. "This is Mia and this is Izzy."

"Hi," the Cherubics said shyly to the older angels.

They all took their seats and Gabrielle looked at what was going on around her. All the angels appeared to be waiting for permission to eat, so she did the same.

Angel Fleur, who was sitting at the top table with the other teachers, placed a napkin on her knee, nodded, and took a mouthful of food. The meal began.

Gabrielle felt as though she hadn't eaten for a month and she tucked into her food heartily.

"Gabrielle Divine, sit up straight and take time with your food!" said a squeaky voice.

"It's Angel Patsy, the meal monitor," said Ruth. "She's in an even worse mood now than she was at lunchtime."

Gabrielle saw the small, rounded angel with bouncy, dark bobbed hair thundering towards her. She quickly sat up in her seat and said sorry.

"Oh dear," said Lula. "I hope this amazingly 'special' Earth Angel isn't going to be trouble."

Gabrielle was taken aback by Lula's snide comment.

Izzy and Mia giggled, but no one else at the table was amused.

Ruth quickly changed the subject.

"So, what's the first charm we can get for our bracelets?" she asked.

"It's the Chevalange Charm," said Charity, knowledgeably. "We can get it by the end of term if we work really hard. The first task is Chevalange Care!"

"Sounds fun!" said Hope.

"Yeah, sounds okay, doesn't it, Gabrielle?" said Ruth.

"Erm, yes. Should be great," Gabrielle replied, though she was still distracted by Lula's unexpected comment. The thought of the first charm was certainly thrilling, but suddenly she felt strangely uncomfortable.

Ruth smiled at Gabrielle kindly and moved in to whisper: "Sylvie says Lula has failed to earn her Caring Arts Charm twice, apparently. Wonder why?"

Gabrielle smiled. Thank goodness she had Ruth to look out for her.

Chapter 7

While the other angels at Angel Academy
had been flying all their lives, Gabrielle
had only just started and was determined
to catch up. It was a wonderful sensation
to be able to float through the air, but she
didn't trust herself yet to do anything
more than flutter close to the ground.

After the first few days she was finally
allowed outside to fly around the gardens.

She hoped that one day she might circle the
whole school, rising high above the turrets.
But for now, she was still a bit shaky and
found that she misjudged her speed and
made some rather bumpy landings. As she
settled into Angel Academy, it was gradually
becoming more natural to her though.

One day, between classes,
she floated out to
the gardens and
started to fly
towards a small
clump of trees. Things seemed
to be going well, so she picked up
speed. But the trees appeared in front of her
sooner than she expected.

Gabrielle performed a clumsy sideways
move and narrowly avoided crashing into

them. "Phew! That was close!" she said,
to no one in particular.

"Yeah, try looking ahead and flying at the
same time," said a familiar voice from below.

It was Lula. She and her friends were
watching from a little wooden bench. They
fell about laughing at Gabrielle, mimicking
the way she had steered away from the
trees.

Gabrielle hated the others making fun of
her, and floated back to Crystals miserably,
with the sound of their laughter ringing in
her ears.

There was no one else in Crystals
when she got safely back, so Gabrielle sat
down and wrote a letter to her parents,
telling them that she was unique as an
Earth Angel. *I wish I'd known I was a one-off,*

but it's amazing to be so special, she wrote.
*And I can fly a bit already. But I'm rubbish
at it!*

Gabrielle felt embarrassed that she hadn't
been flying all of her life like the other
Cherubics. But after Lula and her friends
had been so mean, she avoided practising in
the gardens again.

By Thursday of the first week, it was time to
do some work with the chevalanges and
Gabrielle managed to forget her worries
about flying for a while. She was really
looking forward to seeing Domino again.
She'd been so busy that she hadn't managed
to visit him in the paddock since she'd first
arrived.

The new Cherubics met Angel Raphael,

the Chevalange Care teacher, at the stables.

"As you know," said Raphael, "each of you is paired with an angel horse while you are here. Their job is to assist you as you learn your duties as Guardian Angels. The bond that forms between you and your chevalange is an important part of your angelic life. Chevalanges become our dearest friends and they give us the greatest advice. First of all, you need to know how to look after them, and Chevalange Care involves grooming the chevalanges, then learning the correct way to ride on them. Over time, we will develop the way that you and your chevalanges work as a team."

"Yay!" chorused the Cherubics, who all thought the angelic horses they'd been

given on their arrival at Angel Academy
were adorable.

Raphael showed the angels where
the grooming kit and tack were kept and
explained that while there were grooms
to look after the horses at the school, once
the Cherubics became Guardian Angels,
they'd have to look after their chevalanges
themselves.

"Wow!" said Gabrielle. "Look at all this
wonderful stuff!"

There were shelves full of pretty silver
brushes and combs, and accessories for
the chevalanges too; flowers for the
horses' manes, and jewels and fringes
for the bridles. There was a lovely
smell of honeysuckle saddle soap
and beeswax polish.

"You must detangle your chevalange's mane, keep their coats shiny, their hoofs in good condition, and maintain the tack they wear when you ride on them," explained Raphael. "We will begin today by brushing down each chevalange, then shining up their coats, and preparing their manes and tails. On you go!" said Raphael.

The Cherubics didn't need to be told twice. They took baskets crammed full of brushes, fluids and polish, and got to work.

Gabrielle followed each step carefully, chatting to Domino about her first few days at Angel Academy as she worked. It was fun to be able to do something nice for Domino in return for his kindness to her. She washed his coat, dried it and buffed it. Then she applied peppermint and camomile detangling fluid to his mane and tail, and combed them out until they shone.

"There!" she said, once all the work was done. "You look very handsome."

"Thank you, Gabrielle!" Domino said.

Once all the chevalanges looked their best, the angels led them out to the paddock and Angel Raphael showed them how to fit the saddle and bridle. The chevalanges were much larger than earthly horses, and Gabrielle found she had to hover in the air to tack up Domino!

Next to her, Ruth was working on her own chevalange, Humphrey.

"Domino looks lovely, well done!" said Ruth when they'd finished.

"Thanks," said Gabrielle. "And look at Humphrey. He's gleaming!"

They mounted the chevalanges, and walked round the paddock, as Raphael explained how to hold the reins in a way which did not hurt the angel horses.

Gabrielle loved every minute of Chevalange Care and Domino was obviously enjoying himself as well. All too soon the lesson came to an end.

"It's time to head back," said Raphael. "Well done, Cherubics!"

After the lesson, Angel Raphael came to see Gabrielle. "Well done, Gabrielle," he said. "You're a natural at this!"

"Thank you," said Gabrielle, wishing that learning to fly would come so easily as learning how to work with Domino!

Chapter 8

The first week at Angel Academy passed in a flash. It was Friday teatime already and Gabrielle felt as though she had lived at the Academy for ever. She missed her parents terribly, but life was so fast-moving and there was so much to learn and enjoy, that she didn't have time to feel homesick.

As she sat with her new friends at their table in the Ambroserie – well away from

Lula, who had chosen another group to sit with now – a bell tinkled. This had never happened at tea before. Gabrielle looked around curiously to see what was going on. Everyone fell silent.

Madame Seraph rose up from the top table and hovered in the centre of the Ambroserie. "Those of you who are new may not realize that we hold a brief meeting each Friday teatime, just before dessert. We celebrate our weekly achievements and also highlight unfortunate offences against the school rules. In addition, I give out general notices about school life. Starting on a positive note, we would like to make the following awards:

"To our Head Girl, Katie Clouds, we

award the 'Angel of the Week' moonstone brooch," said Madame Seraph. "Katie has done particularly well in the Caring Arts this week."

Katie stood up and collected the brooch from the Head Angel, while the other pupils cheered. She was a sweet-looking angel, with round, honest eyes and rosy cheeks.

"Katie will wear the brooch for a week, and then someone else will win the privilege. So, it's something for you all to aspire to," said Madame.

Gabrielle thought how wonderful it would be to wear the moonstone brooch.

"Moving on," Madame continued, "the next award is for 'Cherubic Who Made the Most Progress'. It's very well deserved and I am delighted to announce that it goes to Gabrielle Divine, who has met the challenge of being a little different from the rest of us with great enthusiasm and sparkle. She wins a basket of angelic goodies for her room. Please come forward to collect it, Gabrielle."

"Me?" said Gabrielle, stunned at being the centre of attention, whilst her room-mates cheered and whooped along with the other trainee angels.

Ruth had to push her off her chair and practically lead Gabrielle up to Madame Seraph to receive the basket of treats. She saw that it contained talcum powders, bubble baths, creams and soaps, plus notebooks, pens and peppermint drops.

Gabrielle blushed bright pink and thanked Madame Seraph.

Once the Ambroserie had settled again, Madame resumed her talk. She told off two girls for being seen in the corridor after lights out, and another angel for failing to complete a piece of homework. Each of those in trouble was to be denied Saturday hobbies.

After dessert, when the teachers had left, Gabrielle lifted her basket proudly and, even though she could hardly see over it, made her way to the exit with her friends. As she walked past Lula's table, she didn't see Lula stand up and move her chair out and she crashed right into it!

"Aaargh!" cried Gabrielle, as she tripped over the chair and catapulted headlong over Lula's table. The contents of the basket flew up into the air in a messy explosion of talcum powder, hand cream and flying peppermint drops.

"Oops, sorry! Was that my fault?" said Lula, while everyone in the Ambroserie collapsed in fits of giggles.

Gabrielle lay across the table with a dusting of talc all over her. She began to cough and splutter. The nearest angel to her was Merry Harper, who came across to help. Ruth and the twins came to Gabrielle's rescue immediately too, setting her on her feet and placing all the goodies back into the basket.

Gabrielle wished she could believe that it had been an unfortunate accident, but she was sure Lula had done it on purpose.

The older angel didn't seem sorry at all.

* * *

In Crystals later that evening, Gabrielle and Ruth were trying out halo hairstyles at their dressing tables while the twins wrote letters home.

"Thanks for coming to save me in the Ambroserie earlier, Ruth," said Gabrielle. "It's so nice to have you on my side."

"That's what friends are for," Ruth smiled.

"I can't believe I tripped like that," said Gabrielle. "I'm such a clumsy klutz."

"It wasn't your fault," said Ruth. "Lula pushed back her chair on purpose. I'm sure of it."

"Do you think Lula doesn't like me?" asked Gabrielle.

"Everyone likes you," said Ruth.

"I don't think Lula does," said Gabrielle.

"Maybe she's just jealous because you're different," said Ruth.

"But I wish I was like everyone else," said Gabrielle sadly. "There's nothing to be jealous about. I might have won the Progress Award but I'm not as good at flying as everyone else and I hate practising now, especially since Lula laughed at me in the gardens. I don't think I'll ever be able to fly properly. And if I can't fly, how can I be a Guardian Angel?"

Ruth was quiet for a moment. "I know what," she whispered, so the twins couldn't hear. "Why don't we sneak out later and practise flying skills with no one around?"

"Oh, I'm not sure," said Gabrielle.

"We're not supposed to do that, are we?"

"Go on. No one will ever know and you won't have to worry about anyone watching. It'll be fun and I'll give you some flying tips," said Ruth.

Oh, what should I do? thought Gabrielle. It seemed like a great idea – less embarrassing than making flying mistakes in daylight and she really did want to be able to fly like the other angels.

"It's completely up to you," said Ruth.

"Well, I suppose so," said Gabrielle. "I could do with some tips."

"We'll wait until the twins are asleep and creep out quietly," said Ruth.

Gabrielle bit her lip. Ruth's idea sounded really helpful, but very worrying too.

Chapter 9

After lights-out that night, the school
fell into a silent, dreamy sleep. It wasn't
an inky black night, but a gentle blue
twilight that fell over the town of Bliss.
Ruth and Gabrielle were still wide awake
– in fact they hadn't even changed into
their nightclothes.

Luckily, Hope and Charity had fallen
asleep very quickly.

"Let's go!" whispered Ruth.

"Okay," said Gabrielle, getting out of bed, and pulling her velvet cloak around her shoulders.

Even though she had worried about Ruth's plans, she found herself getting carried along on the wave of excitement and she couldn't wait to set off on their flying adventure.

Ruth opened the creaky door of their room. Gabrielle was convinced she heard Sylvie tutting her disapproval from the windowsill, but she tried to ignore her and the girls tiptoed down the hallway to the main door.

It was locked.

"Now what?" said Gabrielle, terrified that they would activate some kind of trumpet alarm which would waken the whole school. She could just imagine Lula Spendlove's smug face if that happened.

"I don't know," said Ruth. "I'm trying to remember where the other exits are. Let's try this way." She turned in the opposite direction.

Finally they came to a small unlocked back door, which opened onto the fragrant floral courtyard.

"Perfect," said Ruth. Gabrielle felt her heart fluttering as she left the school building. She was breaking the rules, when all she really wanted to do was impress Madame Seraph and be the best angel she could be. But it would surely be worth it when she finally learned to fly properly.

"Where are we going to fly?" asked

Gabrielle, hoping they wouldn't get caught.

"Just around the grounds," said Ruth.

"Okay, but don't go too fast – I've never flown in the dark before!" said Gabrielle.

"Don't worry. All you need to do is learn to judge speed and space," said Ruth.

Gabrielle liked hearing about flying from someone who'd been doing it all her life.

"Come on," said Ruth. "Float up with me and we'll do some turns."

Gabrielle followed Ruth's lead and they flew to the east, then the west, gradually going faster and getting higher.

"Wheee! This is fun!" called Gabrielle.

"You're actually very good when you relax!" said Ruth. "We'll try a low swoop now. Just do as I do. Your wings will take your weight, you only have to steer."

At first, Gabrielle could not get the hang of flying low over the ground, then rising high into a soar. But Ruth showed her how to use the position of her arms and head to help her steer and balance, and the next time, Gabrielle concentrated really hard.

She dived downwards, then with a few metres left between herself and the ground, she pointed her arms and head upwards and felt herself racing high into the sky. It was the greatest feeling, and much less nerve-wracking under the cover of darkness than it was in daylight.

"You're getting so good, perhaps we could swoop and soar over the lake? It looks beautiful from the air," said Ruth, after they'd flown around the Angel Academy grounds several times.

"That sounds brilliant. But it might be a bit dangerous. I'm only just getting the hang of flying. What if I fall in?" Gabrielle asked anxiously.

"You won't fall in, I promise you. You've got great balance and control now," said Ruth.

"It does sound amazing…" Gabrielle was still unsure.

"Come on, follow me," said Ruth.

They flew across the gardens and approached the edge of the moonlit lake.

"Are you ready?" asked Ruth.

"Erm, I think so," said Gabrielle.

The water was like a mirror and the light from the stars sparkled mesmerizingly on its surface. Side by side, the girls swooped over the lake at full speed.

"Wheee! I love this!" called Gabrielle.

"I told you it would be fun. You're great at this," said Ruth.

Gabrielle had no fear of falling. This was just what she had needed; some extra practice with no one laughing at her. "It feels like a beautiful dream," she said, caught up in the thrill of the starlit angel world. She completely forgot that they were breaking the rules; it was all so magical. Nothing like this had ever happened at home. That other world seemed a distant, fuzzy memory already.

Gabrielle tried flying low, just above the water. She loved the sense of control. She threw her head from side to side, feeling the wind in her hair and…

"Oh no!" she cried. "My halo has fallen into the lake." Gabrielle panicked. Her halo was just about her most important possession, as it gave her most of her angelic powers. It was unthinkable that she could survive at Angel Academy without it.

"I must find it!" she cried, diving into the lake.

SPLASH!

"Gabrielle, no!" called Ruth urgently from the night sky.

But Gabrielle was already in the lake, bobbing on the surface of the water. She looked around and saw her halo floating close by, giving off a bright light. She swam over and grabbed it, calling out: "Got it!"

"Gabrielle, get out of the water. Now!" called Ruth.

Something in the tone of Ruth's voice alarmed Gabrielle. She swam to the edge of the lake and looked up.

Oh no! Help!

Madame Seraph's chevalange Portia was hovering in the air above her and sitting on the horse's back was the Head Angel herself. She looked extremely angry!

Chapter 10

Huddled on the lakeside, Gabrielle was shivering with cold. Her lovely angel gown and cloak dripped with water, and her hair was a crazy wet mess. She'd hastily put her halo back on her head but it kept slipping to one side.

"You disappoint me, angels," said Madame Seraph as she dismounted gracefully from Portia. "Gabrielle!

Swimming in the lake? What were you thinking?"

"I'm s-s-so sorry," stammered Gabrielle, suddenly feeling queasy as it dawned on her how serious the situation was. "My halo fell in."

"And how did that happen?" asked Madame Seraph.

"It was my fault," said Ruth. "All of this is my fault. I offered to help Gabrielle with learning to fly. She gets embarrassed when she's being watched. Blame me."

"I am not interested in blame. I am concerned about your personal responsibility. I did not expect this of you, Gabrielle Divine. I am shocked by your appalling behaviour. You have both let me down. It's a good job that Sylvie told

Portia you'd gone out." Madame Seraph was furious.

"You are my children while you are at Angel Academy. I am trusted by your parents to look after you. This is terrible conduct. Simply terrible. And Gabrielle, you've only been flying for a matter of days. I feel faint when I think what could have happened to you! But we must get you indoors. Portia will take us back to school." Madame Seraph's jet-black chevalange stood nearby, looking on curiously.

Gabrielle and Ruth shuddered. What had seemed like a brilliant idea suddenly seemed very stupid. Madame Seraph mounted Portia and the girls climbed on behind her. The chevalange flew over the lake majestically and, within minutes, landed at the school.

Once they were inside the building, Madame Seraph saw the girls safely back to their room.

"You will be called to my office immediately after breakfast tomorrow. Do you have anything to say before I send you to bed?" she asked.

"Please forgive me," said Gabrielle.

"I'm very sorry that I suggested this to Gabrielle, Madame Seraph," whispered Ruth. "But I only wanted to help her."

Madame shook her head. "Dry off well and get some sleep," she said. "Goodnight, Cherubics."

Once they were inside Crystals, both girls hung their halos on their bedside stands and began to sob softly.

"I'm sorry I had to tell, girls," said Sylvie from the windowsill. "But I was worried about you."

"It's okay, Sylvie," said Gabrielle. "We understand."

Gabrielle was freezing now and she took off her angel clothes, dried herself with a fluffy towel, and changed into her nightclothes. Her white angel gown and velvet cloak were ruined. What kind of madness had come over her – to dive into the lake, wearing the gown she had dreamed of for so long?

"This is all my fault," said Ruth. "I'm an idiot. I'm so sorry."

"It's my fault too," said Gabrielle. "But

I bet I'll be in more trouble than you. I was the one in the lake in my brand new angel clothes – and we only went flying because of me. What if I get expelled? How will I tell my parents? I've never broken any rules before."

"Oh my goodness. Expelled?" said Ruth. "Do you think so? Maybe we'll both have to leave!"

"I will never be able to forgive myself," said Gabrielle, brushing hot, prickly tears from her weary eyes.

"I wish I could turn the clock back," said Ruth sadly. "We should never have gone out."

Gabrielle hardly slept that night. Her mind was whooshing round in circles with terrible, unsettling thoughts, like a washing machine on a fast spin. *What if I'm sent home? I'll never be able to earn my charms! What will Mum and Dad say?*

Gabrielle had never felt so upset. She was growing to love life at Angel Academy and the thought of having to leave now was unbearable.

Chapter 11

The next morning, Gabrielle forced herself
out of bed, feeling exhausted and tense.
The terrible events from the night before
hit her afresh and she almost collapsed
as the details came flooding back. The first
week at Angel Academy had been so much
fun. But to end it like this…!

She showered and tied her hair back in
a severe ponytail. She had no thoughts of

pretty hairstyles now. She put on her pale turquoise gown.

I'm sure to get into masses of trouble, she thought, as she trudged down to breakfast with Ruth, Charity and Hope.

"What's up with you?" Charity asked. "You look terrible!"

It was nice to have a room-mate who was very straight and to the point, but this morning Charity was a little too direct.

"Leave her alone," said Ruth. "You can see that Gabrielle's upset."

"Sorreee," said Charity. "I only wanted to help."

"No one can help," said Gabrielle. "I've been caught breaking the school rules, and I'm going to find out my punishment from Madame Seraph today."

"What? I don't get it. You just got a Progress Award at tea yesterday. What are you talking about?" said Charity.

"It's my fault," explained Ruth. "We went flying after lights-out last night and we're both in big trouble. But it's worse for Gabrielle, because she dived into the lake to rescue her halo and Madame found her in there."

"That's bad luck," said Charity.

If Madame Seraph gives me another chance, I will never let her or myself down like this again, Gabrielle vowed silently.

Breakfast should have been a delicious feast, but Gabrielle only managed a glass of fresh cranberry juice as her tummy was doing somersaults and she had no appetite.

After breakfast, a trumpet sounded and

weekend hobbies were due to begin. An assistant asked Gabrielle to go to Madame Seraph's study immediately.

"Good luck," said Ruth, giving Gabrielle a quick hug. "It'll be my turn next."

Gabrielle made her way along the almost-familiar corridors, feeling very nervous.

She sat anxiously outside Madame Seraph's office, clasping and unclasping her hands, and fiddling with her bracelet.

The assistant called Gabrielle into the study. It seemed to be empty, but Madame Seraph appeared on her chair before them.

"Gabrielle Divine," said Madame Seraph. "You have no idea how much I have looked forward to your arrival here. For many years, the thought of your training has been on my mind. You show great promise. But this is a disastrous start, to say the very least. I simply do not know if you can carry on here under the circumstances – for your own safety."

Gabrielle winced. "I'm ashamed of myself," she said. "I don't know what came over me, but I will never do anything dangerous again. I take full responsibility for breaking the rules and do not blame Ruth."

"That is in your favour, Gabrielle," said Madame Seraph. "Even so, you leave me in a very difficult position today. You see, your differences make you extra-special, and we have such high hopes for you. I don't want to have to send you away but, in theory, I should expel you with immediate effect."

Gabrielle swallowed hard. Could her dream really all be over so soon? *Please give me another chance,* she pleaded silently.

"You have shown that you cannot be trusted – the most shaming flaw for an angel. You are in my care and if any harm comes to you, I am responsible. Do you understand the seriousness of what you did?" said Madame Seraph.

"Yes," Gabrielle whispered.

Madame Seraph sighed and played with the rose quartz beads around her neck, as if taking inspiration from their smooth, glassy surface. Gabrielle watched her closely, with her heart pounding in her chest.

"Here's what we'll do," said Madame Seraph finally. "You have until Parents' Day to prove to me that you are worthy of

Cherubic status. We will call this a trial period. I am making an allowance for you now, as your reason for breaking the rules was not wrong in itself. I know that your intentions were good, and that you and Ruth were simply trying to improve your flying, but at Angel Academy we insist that you respect the rules. They are there for a purpose – to protect you. Now do you have any questions?"

"Will you tell my parents?" Gabrielle asked.

"I must, but I will cause them the minimum anxiety I can," said the Head Angel. "But from now on your behaviour must be perfect. Any lapse will result in immediate expulsion, which would break my heart and perhaps yours too. Now,

I suggest you have a quiet morning of
reflection, then join the others at lunch."

"Thank you, Madame Seraph. I will not
let you down," said Gabrielle. "I give you
my word."

Gabrielle felt relieved that she had been
given a chance to redeem herself, but was
still thoroughly ashamed. She was glad it
was Saturday and there were no classes.
She went to discuss her feelings with
Domino straight away.

The chevalange was bathing in
sunlight in the paddock when
he saw Gabrielle approach.

"Ah, I'm glad you've come," he said.

"You did say I could discuss anything
with you, didn't you?" she said.

He nodded.

"Well, I've been an idiot."

"Yes, you have, little angel. I've heard all about it from Portia," he said. "You were very silly, but I know your intentions were good."

"Yes. And I'll never do anything like that again," she replied.

"You simply cannot – if you want to stay here," he said.

"Of course I do," said Gabrielle.

"I see great promise in you, Angel Gabrielle. I'm sure we have many exciting adventures ahead of us," said Domino in his comforting, velvety voice.

"You think I can still do really well here? And earn my Angel Charms?"

"Yes," smiled Domino. "But you will

have to use all your wisdom and sense over the coming weeks."

"I will, I promise," she said, allowing herself a little smile. "Thank you, Domino!"

When Gabrielle got back to Crystals, a new gown and cloak had been delivered for her, exactly like those she had ruined in the lake.

Ruth couldn't wait to speak to Gabrielle.

"I'm in heaps of trouble," said Ruth. "I'm on a trial period. How about you? We guessed you wouldn't need another gown if you were leaving. But you've got one! Does that mean you're staying? Are we right? Are we? Please say yes!"

"I'm on a trial period too – perfect behaviour until Parents' Day," said Gabrielle. "Or else I have to go."

"Same here," said Ruth. "I promise I won't be having any more crazy ideas!"

"I honestly thought it was all over," said Gabrielle. "I'm so relieved."

"Me too," said Ruth. "I really thought I'd hate it here. I was so determined to be different from everyone else in my family. But when Madame told me I could be expelled, I realized how much I wanted to stay. And now that we're such good friends, there's no way I could bear to be anywhere else!"

"Snap," said Gabrielle, hugging her friend. But she knew the pressure was on, and that she couldn't afford to make even the smallest mistake or she'd be sent home in disgrace.

Chapter 12

By Monday, Gabrielle had recovered a
little, and she decided to focus on the
future as much as possible, even though
the "trial period" was always on her mind.
The entire school was getting together
to rehearse an airborne dance routine for
Parents' Day. The older angels were
instructed to help the Cherubics learn the
skills needed to Angelfly.

Gabrielle and her room-mates were excited.

"I can't wait to see how it's done," said Hope.

"What exactly is 'Angelfly'?" asked Gabrielle.

"It's sort of ballet in the air," said Ruth. "But when you get really good, you can fly as a group of angels, in formation, moving perfectly in time with one another. It's ever so hard to get right, but absolutely beautiful to watch."

"Oooh, it sounds so exciting!" said Gabrielle.

The girls headed off for the meeting point in the gardens.

In the corridor on the way out, Lula, Mia and Izzy brushed past Gabrielle and Ruth.

"So, the Earth Angel thinks she's a mermaid," said Lula unkindly. "Have you dried off yet?"

Gabrielle ignored her. She had dreaded bumping into Lula since the disastrous midnight lake incident.

"What's her problem?" said Ruth.

"I wish I knew what I'd done to annoy her, then I could try to put things right," said Gabrielle.

Out on the lawns, the Angelfly teacher, Angel Anna, waited for them.

"Cherubics, one of the marks of a Guardian Angel from this Academy is her ability to Angelfly. Watch carefully as the older angels perform for you. They will demonstrate the float and the spin – very easy moves to do. Then we will put each of you in a group with some of the older girls and you can try the moves for yourselves."

Gabrielle watched with awe as the more senior angels floated gracefully up into the air and began to hover above them, arms outstretched. Then they spun round and round in ever-changing formations, with their gowns and wings fluttering around them. Their halos sparkled in the morning sun and the Cherubics were dazzled by the light – and by the sparkling performances. They couldn't wait to get started.

Angel Anna floated among the trainees and told each angel which of the older groups they should join.

"Ah, Gabrielle," she said. "Lovely to meet you. Now, as I know you're new to flying, I'm going to put you with Lula, Izzy and Mia; they're excellent Angelfly dancers. You'll be in very safe hands. Good luck!"

Gabrielle froze for a moment. All the excitement was crushed out of her by the thought of being in Lula's group.

"Gabrielle, are you okay?" said Angel Anna.

"Erm, yes. I'll just, erm, join my group," she said.

"Good luck!" called Ruth, sympathetically.

When she flew over to Lula and the others, Gabrielle thought she heard the faintest tut of disappointment from Lula.

"I'm sorry I won't be very good," said Gabrielle. "I've only been flying for a few days."

"But you are 'exceptional', aren't you?

So you shouldn't have a problem. Come on, let's get on with it," said Lula. "Follow us into the air and then we'll show you how to float and spin."

The little group of angels flew up into the air and hovered above the gardens.

"So, the way we float is that we stretch out our arms and lie horizontally, with our faces looking down to the ground," explained Lula.

Gabrielle did exactly as Lula said and found it surprisingly easy.

"Oh. So you can do that," said Lula. "Spins are a little more difficult. You point your feet downwards and keep your arms close to your body. Tilt your head to the left and you will turn a little. You need to propel yourself round and round, but don't move your arms…"

"But…" said Mia.

"Ssshh," said Lula. "I'm teaching her."

Gabrielle tried her best to rotate, but found this move very difficult with her arms tucked into her body. She looked over to the other trainees, who seemed to be using their arms to help them.

"Come on, try it again," said Lula.

The three older angels laughed as Gabrielle lost height and began to plummet towards the ground at great speed, with her limbs flailing in different directions.

"Help!" she cried out. "Help me!"

Angel Anna realized that Gabrielle was in freefall. "Use your arms to balance and steady yourself, Gabrielle," she called.

"And your wings too!"

Just before she reached the ground, Gabrielle managed to find her balance and fly evenly again, but she had lost her nerve and landed in the gardens, all of a flutter.

"What went wrong, Gabrielle?" asked Angel Anna. "You must use your arms during the spin."

"But—"Gabrielle began. She was going to say that Lula had told her the exact opposite, then she decided not to tell tales on Lula.

"Try to listen to the instructions more closely," said Angel Anna.

"I'm sorry. I will concentrate more carefully in future," said Gabrielle. She looked over to Lula, Mia and Izzy. All three had very red faces and could not meet her eye.

Gabrielle was disappointed that her first Angelfly session had not gone better. She had so wanted to make a good impression.

But there was no time to think about her worries, because Katie Clouds suddenly wailed: "My brooch! It's gone missing!"

"What do you mean?" said Angel Anna. "Did it fall off?"

"Yes, I think so, while I was doing Angelfly. I've looked all around for it, but I can't see it anywhere!" Katie was distraught.

Angel Anna asked everyone to search the lawn for Katie's "Angel of the Week" moonstone brooch. But it was nowhere to be seen. Gabrielle remembered how awful it had felt to lose her halo temporarily, and she was deeply sorry for Katie.

* * *

At lunch, Ruth asked Gabrielle what had happened to her during Angelfly.

"I feel such an idiot. I got all muddled up," said Gabrielle.

She paused for a moment, then decided to tell the truth. "Lula told me to keep my arms close to my body."

"Why would she say that? You need to use your arms. You could have had a very nasty accident!" said Ruth crossly. "She really is too mean to be an angel!"

"Surely she wouldn't want to hurt me?" said Gabrielle.

"She certainly seems to have it in for you," said Ruth.

After lunch, the two girls headed back to their room to collect some books for afternoon classes. When they arrived

back at Crystals, Sylvie was waiting
on the windowsill to welcome them.

"I heard about your
Angelfly lesson. Don't worry,
Gabrielle, you'll be brilliant at
it soon!" said Sylvie.

"Thanks, Sylvie," said Gabrielle.

"And here's something to cheer you
up," said Sylvie. "A letter from home!"

Gabrielle ran to take the envelope
from Sylvie.

"Yippee! It's Mum's writing!" she
said. Gabrielle was very excited but
she was also a little worried about what
Mum and Dad would say about the trial
period. She tore into the envelope and
took in the soft, delicate fragrance of
her mother.

Darling Gabrielle,

I was thrilled to receive the first letter from you. I am so terribly sorry (but very proud) that you are the only Earth Angel at school. I didn't realize that we were both so unusual! And I can't believe that you're flying already. You mustn't worry about being a bit behind with it — after all, you've never flown before and the others have.

Another letter arrived last night. It was from Madame Seraph. About the trial period! Dad and I were very surprised, as it's not like you to break the rules, but I'm sure there is a good explanation. We hope nothing like that ever happens again! I am glad that Madame is watching over you carefully.

I am so looking forward to Parents' Day, sweetheart. Not long now. Dad and I are *missing you very much. Not knowing what Angel Academy is like makes us miss you all the more. Please tell me more about it in your next letter. Be your own lovely angelic self and I'm sure all will be well.*

See you soon
Love you,
Mum XX
P.S. Dad says the same.

Gabrielle sobbed into her pillow – lovely Mum and Dad! She missed them too, especially at the moment, and she felt so ashamed about being on the trial period. *I just don't know how I could have messed up so badly,* she thought.

Ruth came over and put her arm around Gabrielle. "Cheer up," she said. "By

Parents' Day this whole trial thing will be over, and you'll wonder what you were worried about."

"Yes, I'm sure you're right," said Gabrielle.

Chapter 13

Before she knew it, Parents' Day was
only one day away. *Almost the end of the trial
period*, thought Gabrielle. Before classes,
Gabrielle and her room-mates
busily tidied their room and sorted their
clothes. Everything had to be perfect for
the next day.

In the afternoon, the girls had a lesson
in Potion-making with Angel Blossom.

"To begin with, we will make a Comfort Potion – ideal for a human suffering from shock or stress. A drop of this left on their pillow by an invisible Guardian Angel will do a power of good!"

Gabrielle couldn't wait to start mixing the ingredients: violet, lavender, cloves, vanilla and lime. She soon got the hang of taking a little extract of each scent in a pipette, and dropping it into a glass vial of distilled water.

The afternoon passed in a fragrant flash, and after Potion-making, the girls enjoyed a delicious tea in the Ambroserie. As it was a Friday, Madame made her usual announcements and read out a long list of instructions about Parents' Day. Then she made a special appeal.

"As you know, Katie still has not found the 'Angel of the Week' moonstone brooch and until she does we cannot award it to anyone else, which is deeply distressing for all of us. If anyone has any idea what has happened to it, please let me know," said Madame Seraph.

"Poor Katie must be feeling awful," said Gabrielle. "I thought it would have turned up by now."

Everyone agreed it was very bad luck, and for a while Gabrielle's table fell silent. But then the halo cakes arrived, and the angels couldn't help but cheer up.

Gabrielle had never tried halo cakes before. The golden honey buns were filled with syrup and topped with delicious white icing.

"We should make this a celebration tea," said Ruth, helping herself to a second cake.

"What do you mean?" said Gabrielle.

"Well, we'll both be off the trial period from tomorrow," said Ruth.

"Shouldn't we hold on until we know for sure?" said Gabrielle. She couldn't wait to be free of that worry – and to see Mum and Dad. She hoped Parents' Day was going to be wonderful.

Back in Crystals, Gabrielle ran a bubble bath and wallowed in it for a while.

As she poured some more cherry blossom bath oil into the water, she heard a commotion out in the room. *What's going on?* she wondered, straining to hear the voices, which sounded rather tense.

"Oh no! What's it doing in there?" she heard Charity say.

"I'm sure she didn't put it there," said Ruth. "She'd never do anything like that."

"I agree it's unlike her."

Is that Angel Fleur's voice? thought Gabrielle.

She became more curious and got out of the bath, drying herself quickly. She tied her towelling robe around herself and wrapped up her hair in a fluffy towel.

Gabrielle emerged from the bathroom. "What's going on?" she asked. She stopped in her tracks when she saw Angel Fleur and her room-mates peering into her bedside cabinet.

Every face in the room turned to stare at

her with a mixture of pity and shock.

"Tell me. What is it?" said Gabrielle falteringly.

Angel Fleur moved towards her. "Gabrielle, Madame received an anonymous note after tea, saying that the moonstone brooch had been stolen and hidden in a Cherubic dorm. And I've been making an inspection of all the trainees' rooms. I'm afraid I've found the brooch in the bottom drawer of your cabinet."

Gabrielle was silent for a moment. She felt confused. The "Angel of the Week" moonstone brooch in her cabinet? It couldn't be so!

At last she found her voice. "NO!" she wailed. "I didn't put it there! You know I'd never do anything like that! Please believe me! I don't know how it got there."

She felt her legs wobble beneath her and the room began to spin. She sat down on the floor with a bump. Someone must have played a terrible trick on her. But how could she prove that she was innocent?

"Be strong, Gabrielle. We know you'd never take the brooch," said Ruth. "You have to fight this. Someone must have sneaked into the room and put it in your cupboard to make you look guilty – whoever wrote that letter to Madame must have done it. We have to find out who it was."

Gabrielle got to her feet. Her face was ashen and her expression pained. She looked to Angel Fleur for guidance.

"I'm sorry, Gabrielle, but I will have to take the brooch to Madame Seraph and explain where I found it. Do you have anything to say?"

"Just that I didn't take it," whispered Gabrielle, feeling as though all her worst nightmares had come true. She was almost at the end of the trial period, but she would definitely be expelled now. And for something she hadn't done. It was all so hopelessly unfair.

"I don't believe you did it," said Fleur, "and I wish I didn't have to, but I must take you to see Madame Seraph. I'll wait outside while you dress."

Gabrielle dressed shakily, then she turned to Ruth and the twins, who still looked shocked.

"I didn't do it, you must believe me!" she sobbed.

"We do believe you," said Ruth. "There has to be some way we can prove the brooch was put there by someone else!"

"Come along, Gabrielle," said Angel Fleur, from the doorway. "Let's see if we can get to the bottom of this."

"Please help me!" Gabrielle sobbed.

"We'll do all we can, I promise!" said Ruth, hugging her friend.

Gabrielle floated along to Madame Seraph's study on a cloud of despair. She could not lift her eyes from the floor. Being caught outside in the lake out of hours was bad enough, but this was easily the most terrible thing that had ever happened to her. *Stealing is something I'd never do! This is all so unfair,* she thought.

Gabrielle and Fleur went into Madame

Seraph's study. The Head Angel was already at her desk.

"Gabrielle?" said Madame, looking puzzled.

"I will try to explain," said Angel Fleur. She told Madame where the moonstone brooch had been found.

"Sit down, Gabrielle, please," said Madame Seraph finally.

"Thank you," whispered Gabrielle.

"This is a strange tale indeed," said Madame. "Can you offer an explanation?"

"Madame, I beg you to believe that I did not put the brooch in my cabinet. Someone else must have done it," Gabrielle sobbed.

"But who? Do you have any proof?" said Madame, with a tremble of despair in her voice.

"No. But Ruth and I will work out what happened. Trust me, please," said Gabrielle, suddenly feeling determined to find out the truth.

"But Gabrielle, the problem for me is that you have already stepped out of line. I want to give you another chance, but I am running out of options. If you can prove your innocence before lights-out, then no one will be more delighted than I. But if not, then I'm afraid you will have to leave Angel Academy. Instead of your parents coming here tomorrow, Domino will take you home."

Chapter 14

Gabrielle went back to Crystals with huge, salty tears streaming down her flushed cheeks.

Ruth met her at the door. "Well?" she said.

"We've got until lights-out to prove that I didn't steal the brooch, otherwise I'm leaving before my parents even arrive!" sobbed Gabrielle.

The two friends fell into one another's

arms and held each other close.

"I can't let you go!" said Ruth. "There has to be something we can do. We know you didn't put the brooch there, so who did? There has to be an explanation. Or a witness? Who would have seen someone planting the brooch in here?"

"What about Sylvie?" asked Charity. "Maybe she knows something."

"Yes, of course!" said Ruth, running to the window. "Sylvie! Sylvie! We need you!"

But there was no sign of the little bird.

"Where is she?" asked Ruth.

"I haven't seen her since before Potion-making," said Charity.

"Same here," agreed Hope.

"Well, let's go and find her," said Ruth.

The four room-mates went to ask the

other dove messengers if they'd seen her.

None of them had, so they began to search the school grounds, four Cherubics surrounded by a cloud of gentle doves.

"Sylvie!" they called wherever they went. "Sylvie, where are you?"

They looked in the gardens. Then they looked by the stream. And after that, they searched in the orchards.

"Sylvie!"

"Sylvie!"

"Another mystery," said Charity. "Sylvie is always around. Where can she have gone?"

Ruth stopped in her tracks. "Did you hear that?" she said.

"Hear what?" said Gabrielle.

"It was a little whimper," said Ruth. "Shush, everyone!"

The four girls and the birds who had settled on the branches of nearby trees, fell silent.

"Help!" cried a muffled voice.

It sounded like Sylvie. But where was she?

Ruth followed the sound, which was at ground level. "Sylvie, where are you?" called Ruth.

"In the pink rose bush!" came the reply.

 The whole search party homed in on the bush, pushing back the flowers and leaves. There, in the middle of it, was Sylvie, with a badly injured wing.

"What happened, Sylvie?" asked Gabrielle.

"Oh dear! It was awful!" said the little

bird. "I saw something terrible in Crystals, and I flew to tell Portia, but I couldn't find her. I tried everywhere, and exhausted myself. I collapsed into this bush for a rest. But I've torn my wing on the thorns."

"We're here now, Sylvie, we'll help you!" said Gabrielle.

Sylvie looked upset, and Gabrielle hated to ask her to recall what she'd seen, but it had to be done.

"What was it that upset you so much?" she asked.

"I'll tell you back in Crystals," said Sylvie.

"Come on, I'll carry you," said Ruth, cradling Sylvie in her hands. "We'll try to mend your wing, and you can tell us everything."

To Gabrielle, the walk back to Crystals seemed to last for ever. She tried to be patient, but she was desperate to know what Sylvie had seen.

Chapter 15

Sylvie began to relax once she was back on her favourite windowsill, with a little bandage on her wing.

"After you went to Potion-making, I was sitting here singing, when I heard a noise in the room," she began. "I thought one of you had forgotten something. I peeped inside to see who was there. But it wasn't any of you!"

"Who was it?" gasped Gabrielle.

"It was Lula Spendlove," Sylvie explained.

"What was she doing?" asked Ruth.

"She was kneeling down by Gabrielle's bedside cabinet. She got in all of a fluster when she saw me and she asked me to take a note urgently to the Cherubics in her dorm," said Sylvie. "They weren't there. And when I got back, she was gone. That's when I set off to find Portia."

"That makes sense!" said Ruth. "Lula's been mean to Gabrielle all term and now she's trying to get her into trouble."

Gabrielle felt a bit of hope in her heart for the first time since the moonstone brooch had been discovered.

"Could you bear to come along to Madame Seraph's study with us and tell her what happened? We all know we can trust you. Madame will believe you, for sure," she said.

"Of course I'll come," said Sylvie. "I must stand up for the truth – and for my Cherubics!"

With Ruth at her side, Gabrielle took Sylvie in her hand and they raced down to the Head Angel's study. They paced around as they waited for Madame Seraph's assistant to invite them in.

Finally, they were ushered through and Madame Seraph appeared instantly.

"Oh dear, Sylvie, what has happened to you?" said Madame as soon as she saw the little dove.

"Sylvie should explain everything," said Ruth.

Gabrielle put the bird down on Madame's desk and Sylvie repeated her story.

"I see," said Madame when Sylvie had finished. "I am shocked, I must say. Are you quite sure about this?"

"Yes, I have never been more sure of anything," said Sylvie.

"Well, in that case, wait here while I send for Lula," said Madame Seraph.

As they waited for Lula to appear, Gabrielle hardly dared to hope that her ordeal was over.

Finally, Lula burst into the room, her face flushed. All Gabrielle could think about was why Lula hated her so much. *Why? What have I done to deserve any of this?*

"We want to discuss the missing moonstone brooch," said Madame. "Have you any idea how it ended up in a cabinet in Crystals?"

Lula blushed bright red as soon as she saw Sylvie.

"Erm, no. I went to Crystals to return a pen I found," said Lula.

"Which pen?" Madame Seraph asked.

"Oh, it was one I found in…"

"There was no pen, was there, Lula?" said Madame.

For a while Lula stood silently in the middle of the room, desperately trying to think of an excuse – of some way out. But there was none, and finally she saw that she had to tell the truth. "I'm sorry, Madame," she said at last. "I found the brooch on the lawn after the Angelfly lesson a few weeks ago and I picked it up.

"I was going to hand it in, but then I thought I could use it to accuse Gabrielle of stealing." She looked at the floor. "It took me a while to pluck up the courage to plant the brooch in her cabinet. It was such a foolish thing to do."

"But why did you want to get Gabrielle into trouble?" asked Madame.

"I don't know," said Lula. "Well, I suppose it was because I was jealous of her."

Lula was jealous of her? Gabrielle had never been so shocked. "But what did I do?" she asked Lula.

"Nothing really. It's just, as soon as you arrived, we kept hearing about how special you were, and how you were so exceptional. I've worked really hard the whole time I've been at the Academy, and no one ever gave me an award; no one really seemed to notice. It just didn't seem fair."

"Even so, that was a really mean thing to do," cried Ruth angrily. "What a way to treat an angel who is living in a whole new world for the first time!"

"I'm sorry you felt that way, Lula," said Madame Seraph. "But I'm so ashamed. To think that any of my angels could do such a thing! You might not have won awards, but we gave you so much training and love here, there's no excuse for being so devious and cruel."

"I wasn't thinking," said Lula. "I can see now how wrong it was."

"This is a sorry situation," said Madame. "I promised Gabrielle's parents that she would be cherished here – and now one of my angels does this?"

She floated around the room speedily, as if trying to burn off her anger.

"Ruth, your trial period is lifted – you may go now. And you too, Sylvie," said Madame.

"Thank you," said Ruth.

"Lula, wait outside while I talk to poor Gabrielle," continued Madame.

Lula looked directly at Gabrielle. "I'm very sorry," she said, then with her head bowed she walked out of the door.

"I apologize too, Gabrielle. I should have been able to protect you," said Madame Seraph. "The truth is, you are special to me, but I should not let the others see that so clearly. It's my fault Lula was jealous, not yours. I am delighted to say that your trial period is officially over. Your parents will be very proud of you tomorrow, when they see you flying gracefully around Angel Academy."

Gabrielle felt tears well up in her eyes, she was so relieved. It was as though a miracle had happened. She swallowed hard.

"Thank you, Madame Seraph. You will not regret this decision, I promise," she said.

"I know that," said Madame Seraph with a kind smile. "You may leave now. And enjoy yourself tomorrow!"

Gabrielle flew to tell Domino the good news.

"Ah! So I can go to collect your parents after all!" he said.

"Yes, definitely!" she said, hugging him and smiling happily.

Ruth jumped off her bed as soon as Gabrielle got back to Crystals. "Well, are you allowed to stay?" she asked.

"Yes!" cried Gabrielle, jumping on her bed and bouncing on it.

"Yay! I'm so happy," said Ruth. "Sylvie heard that Lula is being suspended for the rest of this term for what she did! She's gone home already. She's going to miss Parents' Day!"

Sylvie joined all the Cherubics in Crystals in a celebratory dance.

Gabrielle couldn't help feeling sorry for Lula. But it was lovely to think that the older angel wouldn't be troubling her for a while!

Chapter 16

Parents' Day arrived at last. Angel Academy looked dreamy, with garlands of white flowers strung across its enchanting entrance gates. The sound of angelic singing, flutes and harps filled the air, while the aroma of fresh baking came from the school kitchens, where a feast was being prepared.

All the angels looked exquisite in their

best gowns. Gabrielle wore her blush-pink gown for the first time.

"I'll do your hair," said Ruth.

She picked up Gabrielle's brush and set to work. The result was beautiful! Gabrielle's hair was pinned at the sides, while a few delicate curls cascaded over her shoulders. "And now, we just need to place the halo!" said Ruth. She took it from its stand and set it on Gabrielle's head. "There. You're perfect!"

"What would I do without you, Ruth? You're the best friend I could wish for," said Gabrielle.

"And you're mine," said Ruth, flushing a little. "Now, can you do my hair?"

As Gabrielle twisted the last white rosebuds into Ruth's red curls, Angel Fleur came flying through the door of Crystals like a whirlwind.

"Gabrielle, we can see Domino in the air. He's about to land – with your mother and father!"

"Oh, I can't wait to see them," said Gabrielle, with a gulp. She dashed out of the room and onto the front lawn, where she had touched down with Domino just a few weeks before.

It seems like a lifetime ago, she thought as she looked up, her eyes scanning the sky for the majestic sight of Domino approaching.

"Mum! Dad!" she cried, waving crazily as she saw Domino's broad wings soaring overhead, and straining her eyes for her first glimpse of her parents sitting on his back.

When Mum and Dad finally touched down at Angel Academy, Gabrielle realized just how much she had missed them. She ran towards them with outstretched arms and they rushed towards her. They huddled together for a few magical minutes.

"My darling," said Mum.

"Our little angel," said Dad.

"You have wings!" exclaimed Mum.

"I do!" said Gabrielle. "Do you like them?"

"They are magnificent," sobbed Mum.

They hugged each other so tightly, it seemed they were afraid to let go of one another.

But at last, Madame Seraph and Angel Fleur floated by. They smiled kindly and stopped to speak to the Divine family.

"I knew I was right about Gabrielle," Madame told Mum and Dad. "She's very special – and I will always look after her as one of my own."

"Thank you, Madame Seraph," said Mum.

The Divines said goodbye to Domino, who was in need of a rest.

"Let me show you everything," said Gabrielle excitedly.

"I've been waiting to see the Academy for most of my life," said Mum. "It's a dream come true!"

"Come this way," said Gabrielle.

After a tour of the school and grounds, it was time for the Angelfly display.

The new angels flew in circles around the school turrets, with their best gowns

fluttering behind them and
their wings in full angelic
flight. Gabrielle looked
down and saw that Mum and
Dad were watching her with awe.

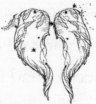

"Gabrielle!" cried Mum, after the
display. "You were faultless. My little girl
can fly! How amazing!"

Gabrielle smiled proudly.

A wonderful feast was laid on in the
Ambroserie, followed by more Angelfly
dancing.

All too soon, it was time for Gabrielle's
parents to go home and it was so hard to
say goodbye.

"I'll be home for Christmas," said
Gabrielle.

"It's a little easier now that I can imagine

you here," said Mum. "But we will miss you every single day."

"Same here," said Gabrielle.

They hugged and Domino coughed gently, reminding them it was time to fly home.

Gabrielle waved until her parents and Domino disappeared. She turned around and looked up at Angel Academy with wonder.

I've survived, she thought. *And whatever lies ahead, I'm sure I can manage it. This is my destiny. I am an Earth Angel and I'm proud of it.*

She heard a familiar chirp. It was Sylvie! Despite her sore wing, she had flown to check that Gabrielle wasn't too sad after seeing off her parents.

"Oh, Sylvie, what a wonderful day!" said Gabrielle. "Let me carry you back to Crystals!"

As they fluttered through the air together, Gabrielle smiled. After all her new experiences and all that had happened over the last few weeks, she was absolutely certain now: Angel Academy was the perfect school for her.

THE END

Gabrielle loves her new life at
Angel Academy.

Turn the page for a divine preview of her
next magical adventure:

Secrets and Surprises

Chapter 1

A flurry of soft snow fell over Angel
Academy, and settled in white pillows on
the rooftops and gardens. Eleven-year-old
Gabrielle Divine had always loved winter
on Earth, but the snow in the angel world
on Cloud Nimbus was even more stunning.

As she gazed out of the window of the
Ambroserie, the Academy's refectory, this
Saturday lunchtime, Gabrielle thought that

the grounds of her new school looked even more beautiful than when she had arrived just a few weeks earlier. She adored living in the magnificent white castle which sat, with its many turrets, towers and curving corridors, on a gentle hill above the angel town of Bliss.

Gabrielle had come to Angel Academy to train to be a Guardian Angel – learning how to protect humans in times of need. She'd been invited to the Academy following the death of her granny: an angel who had fallen in love with and married Gabrielle's granddad, who was human. So Gabrielle was an Earth Angel, which meant that she could live in both the human and the angel worlds. While her parents had not been convinced that she should go to the Academy, Gabrielle had been determined to follow her destiny and, soon after her eleventh birthday, she had set off to join the angel world and learn the skills expected of a Guardian Angel. Since Gabrielle had arrived at the Academy, she'd made some great friends and was constantly finding out new things about the angel world. She had loved every minute of it so far.

Now Gabrielle was sitting at a dining table with her three room-mates, awaiting dessert with excitement.

"Yippee! It's Angel's Fool!" said Gabrielle, as Angel Patsy, the meal monitor carried a tray of delicious, creamy puddings across to them.

The fluffy cream and meringue mixture,

marbled with sweet berries, was a favourite with all the girls and Gabrielle enjoyed each spoonful as she thought about the rest of the day ahead. Saturday afternoon was the best time of the week. There were no lessons, which meant that, along with her room-mates, she always had loads of fun. Today was going to be no exception. In fact, according to her friends, this promised to be one of the best days of the year.

Everyone was fluttering with excitement, because there were now only three weeks of the first term left, and every corridor and room of the school was decorated for the annual angelic festival of Wintervale. There were garlands of green leaves, red berries and silver stars strung across the courtyard at the heart of the ancient Academy, while glowing lanterns hung merrily from the turrets, and apple and cinnamon candles burned sweetly in the alcoves.

"Come on, let's get ready. It's nearly time to go to the Fair!" said Gabrielle's best friend, Ruth Bell, when she'd scraped the last drop of Angel's Fool from her glass bowl.

The students at Angel Academy had been told they could all visit the Wintervale Fair taking place in Bliss that afternoon and Gabrielle was feeling very excited. "I can't wait!" she cried. "It sounds completely magical."

Gabrielle and her three friends floated back to Crystals, the dormitory they shared. Ruth was Gabrielle's very best friend but she loved the twins, Charity and

Hope Honeychurch, too. The twins were ideal room-mates. While Charity was sensible and practical, Hope was dreamy and kind. Ruth was the warmest-hearted girl you could ever wish to know and she was loads of fun too, like the sister Gabrielle had always wanted. *I'm so lucky, having friends like these*, thought Gabrielle.

The four girls rummaged through one another's jewellery boxes, deciding which hair clips and accessories to wear as they brushed their hair and arranged their halos.

"Don't forget," said Charity, "Madame Seraph likes us to look extra smart when we go out of the Academy grounds."

They all wore warm winter gowns at this time of year, made by Angel Willow in the gown department, from layers of the softest pastel-coloured fleece. Some were edged with feather down, while others were decorated with frosty sparkles, and snowflakes embroidered with satin threads. To go outside, they wore cosy velvet cloaks, with large, feather-trimmed hoods, to keep the winter chill from their ears.

When they were all ready, the girls said goodbye to Sylvie, the dainty pink and silver dove who sat on their windowsill, ready to take messages for the girls whenever they needed her. Gabrielle sometimes worried about Sylvie sitting there all alone, but the pretty bird loved her job as messenger and adored the four Cherubics who she helped look after.

"Have a lovely time," said Sylvie.

"Oh, I wish you could come too," said Gabrielle.

"It's too cold out there for me to leave my perch for long!" said Sylvie. "I'm happy to stay here in the warm."

"I know what," said Gabrielle. "I'll buy some soft wool at the Fair – and I'll knit you a stylish beret and scarf to keep you warm this winter!"

"Oooh, I'd love that," said Sylvie. "I've never had a hat or a scarf before!"

"Good! That's agreed then," said Gabrielle.

"Time to go, everyone!" said Charity.

"Bye for now, Sylvie!" called Gabrielle, as she and the others left their cosy dorm.

"Come on. Let's hurry!" said Hope, as the four friends floated along the corridors and out into the snowy landscape. "We don't want to miss anything!"

Gabrielle felt a tingle inside. "Wintervale Fair, here we come!" she cried. "I can't wait!"

The Wintervale Fair is full of lovely surprises, but why is Gabrielle's angel friend, Merry, acting strangely? Find out in:

Secrets and Surprises

Usborne

ANGEL ACADEMY

Secrets and Surprises

Janey Louise Jones

Author of the bestselling Princess Poppy stories

ISBN 9781409538615

If you enjoyed

ANGEL ACADEMY

you might also like:

Silverlake Fairy School

Unicorn Dreams

Lila longs to go to Silverlake Fairy School to
learn about wands, charms and fairy magic –
but spoiled Princess Bee Balm is set on ruining
Lila's chances! Luckily nothing can stop Lila
from following her dreams...

ISBN 9780746076804

Wands and Charms

It's Lila's first day at Silverlake Fairy School, and
she's delighted to receive her first fairy charm and
her own wand. But Lila quickly ends up breaking the
school rules when bossy Princess Bee Balm gets her
into trouble. Could Lila's school days
be numbered...?

ISBN 9780746076811

Ready to Fly

Lila and her friends love learning to fly at
Silverlake Fairy School. Their lessons in the
Flutter Tower are a little scary but fantastic fun.
Then someone plays a trick on Lila and she's
grounded. Only Princess Bee Balm would be so
mean. But how can Lila prove it?

ISBN 9780746090947

Stardust Surprise

Stardust is the most magical element in the
fairy world. Although the fairies are allowed
to experiment with it in lessons, stardust is so
powerful that they are forbidden to use it by
themselves. But Princess Bee Balm will stop
at nothing to boost her magic...

ISBN 9780746076828

Bugs and Butterflies

Bugs and Butterflies is the magical game played at Silverlake Fairy School. Lila dreams of being picked to play for her clan's team, and she's in with a chance too, until someone starts cheating. Princess Bee Balm is also being unusually friendly to Lila... so what's going on?

ISBN 9780746095324

Dancing Magic

It's the end of term at Silverlake Fairy School, and Lila and her friends are practising to put on a spectacular show. There's a wonderful surprise in store for Lila too – one she didn't dare dream was possible!

ISBN 9780746095331

For angels, fairies
and more sparkling stories visit
www.usborne.com/fiction